From the creator of *Dee's B*

WANNA BO

Mark Thunder

Billy is a good old dog
who was good as good can be.

Billy loved his big old bone
and shares it all with me.

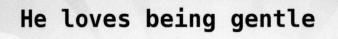

He loves being gentle

but sometimes he plays rough.

When he asks "wanna bone"
The answer is not tough.

Sometimes he burries it
in the spot that is just right.

Sometimes it is soaking wet.
A dogs wet dream delight.

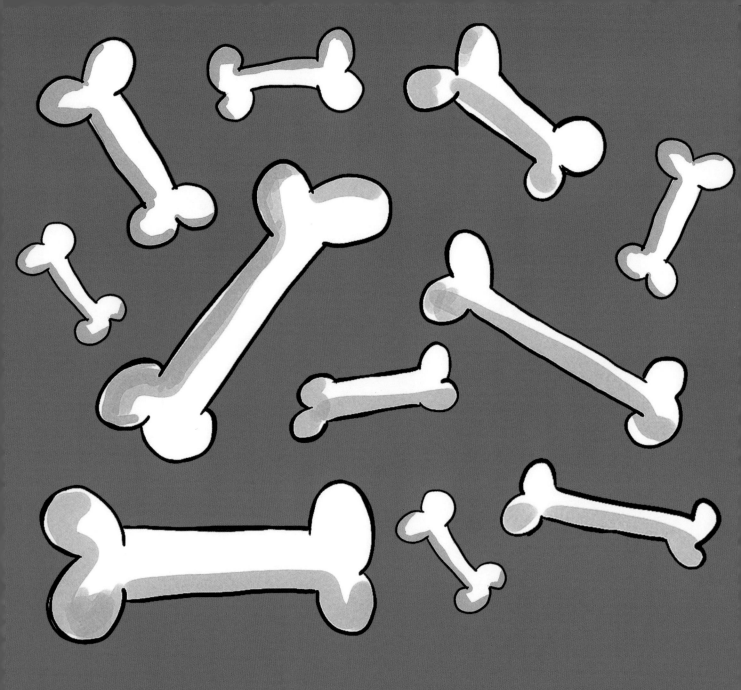

Big bones and small bones,
the bones are quiet a sight.

Sometimes we play with them
all throughout the night.

Sometimes in the morning
when no one is around...

he sneaks into the neighbor's yard
and gives his bone a pound.

Billy pounds it in the garden.
He pounds it in the park.

Sometimes when he's feeling bad,
Billy pounds it in the dark.

People don't believe
the ledgend of its size.

So Billy quickly whips it out,
much to their surprise.

When the weather starts to change
and the last leaf falls...

he puts it in his treasure chest
right next to his blue balls.

But Billy is a good old dog,
who loves his big old bone.

Don't worry in the slightest bit.
He'll enjoy it all alone.

The End.

Check out Mark Thunder's best selling book
Dee's Big Nuts!

DEE'S BIG NUTS

Written by
Mark Thunder

Scan to view on Amazon.com ➔

Printed in Great Britain
by Amazon

34533147R00016